A Chocolate Moose

for Dinner

written and illustrated by
FRED GWYNNE

ALADDIN PAPERBACKS
New York   London   Toronto   Sydney

ALADDIN PAPERBACKS
An imprint of Simon & Schuster Children's Publishing Division
1230 Avenue of the Americas, New York, NY 10020

Originally published by Windmill Books, Inc. and Wanderer Books
ALADDIN PAPERBACKS and colophon are registered trademarks of
Simon & Schuster, Inc.
Designed by Dorothea von Elbe
Manufactured in the United States of America
Second Aladdin Paperbacks edition published January 2005
10 9 8 7 6 5 4 3 2
The Library of Congress has cataloged the hardcover edition as follows:
Gwynne, Fred.
A chocolate moose for dinner.
SUMMARY: A little girl pictures the things her parents talk about, such
as a chocolate moose, a gorilla war, and shoe trees.
ISBN 0-671-6674-6 (hc.)
1. English language—Homonyms—Juvenile literature. [1. English
language—Homonyms. 2. English language—Terms and phrases] I. Title
PE1595.G73 1980   428.1   80-14150
ISBN 0-689-87827-3 (pbk.)

For Keiron, Gaynor, Madyn, Evan, and Furlaud

**Mommy says
she had a
chocolate moose
for dinner last night.**

And after dinner

she toasted Daddy.

there's a gorilla war.

Daddy says
he has trees
for all his shoes.

Daddy says
lions pray on

other  animals.

Daddy says he hates

the arms race.

Daddy says there should

Mommy says her

favorite painter is Dolly.

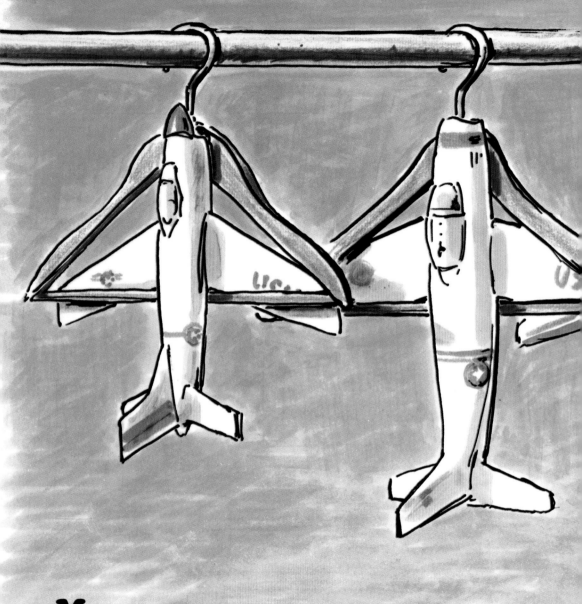

Mommy says there are airplane hangers.

**Daddy says
he has the best
fishing tackle.**

He spent two years in the pen.

And he has just escaped and is now on the lamb.

At the ocean Daddy says

watch out for the under toe.

Daddy says he plays the piano by ear.

Daddy says that in college

people row in shells.

**And some row
in a single skull.**

**Mommy says
she's going to tell me
about Santa Claws.**

And Daddy says he's going to tell me the story of

the tortoise and the hair.

Stories
like these
drive me
up a wall!